Moments of

SIN

"For the wages of sin...is death."

By:

LeMario 'LOKO' Allen

ok online at www.trafford.com
s@trafford.com

titles are also available at major online book retailers.

2010 LeMario 'LOKO' Allen.

oria, BC, Canada.

269-2883-3 (sc)

269-2913-7 (e-book)

*to efficiently provide the world's finest, most comprehensive book publishing
ng every author to experience success. To find out how to publish your book, your
it available worldwide, visit us online at www.trafford.com*

2/24/2010

FForD.   www.trafford.com

This book is dedicated to those who not only inspired,
But encouraged me to go forth with my goals.
Quanese, Vernicia, Thomas...
We've gotten this far, stay with me so we
can reach even higher heights...

Alisha

"Eat that pussy baby." Ebony moaned while I forcefully sucked on her clit.

Growing up as a child I never would have imagined my life to
be like this, but life is full of un-expectations.

bony's thick thighs back, burying my face deep within, marinating my lips with he

Damn that shit taste good." I spoke as her lower lips connected to mine once more
devouring her pussy like a lioness to her prey. She reached over to her nightstand
and removed the more than average sized vibrator from the drawer.

me here baby." She said, placing the dildo on the floor standing at attention in the
"Have a seat sexy." She said, motioning for me to sit down on the artificial dick.

"Ohh fuck." I said, squatting upon it, letting the motion of the
dildo stroke my insides like no real dick ever could.

Ebony stood over me and placed her pussy on top of my face, I had no choice
but to allow my tongue to enter her thick, fleshy folds---beauty in the form
of a pussy, Lord knows I loved it, and could never get enough.

er big toe to click the vibration level of the dildo to its' maximum---I was instantly
alm where I was no longer Alisha; I was just some girl, receiving the pleasure of a l
p and down on the vibrator faster and faster as I ate her with no hesitation. I scre:
as I watched my come coat the vibrator in my hot juices from within. I laid dowr
bony rested on top of me, breathing uncontrollably, trying to get her pulse back to

v long do you think we have to keep sneaking?" Ebony asked, playing with my nir
"I don't know, probably not for too long."
She gave me a kiss and helped me up.

ou might want to hurry and get cleaned up—I already have the hot water running
I pulled her chin towards me and pecked her cheek.

I didn't want my husband to suspect anything…

Latrell

"Damn that ass feels good." I moaned out loud.

"Fuck that ass nigga." Darius demanded.

laid flat on his stomach on the couch and I spread his cheeks for an easier entranc My balls slapped against his ass and made a beautiful rhythm of their own. He ipped tightly on the couch and held for dear life while I tagged that ass like never efore. At this moment I didn't view myself as fucking a man---right now he was m girl and that ass was my pussy. So I took the liberty of treating it just like one.

ass over nigga!" I commanded as he lay on his back with his legs pointing north. s on my shoulders and eased my dick inside. He let his left leg fall but the other re collar bone as I kissed his calves and dicked him down extensively. I went faster, l it all the way inside, watching his hard dick bounce up and down against his sto ke daddy's dick!" I yelled, stroking his dick while he took all 10 ½ inches of min

"You want my babies up in you nigga?" I asked

"Hell yeah, shoot them kids daddy."

He turned me on by encouraging me to nut, so I went harder, stroked him faster until he reached the pinnacle of his climax.

im wildly and watched him skeet all over himself. I pulled out of him and mixec e, coating both of our bodies with hot, sticky remains of what was our moment of n his side and I went behind him and held him, slightly poking his back with my

"Do you love me?" Darius asked

on't start tonight." I said, licking his earlobe and fooling with the g-spot on his nec

"Come on, let's get cleaned up." I offered

icked him up and carried him to the bathroom with the shower running streamin water. I washed him. He washed me, I licked and ate him, and he sucked and dra I helped gather his belongings and assisted in making sure nothing was left behir Everything about our night had to be erased, almost as though it never happened.

I opened the door for him and he stepped out. I called his name and he turned around, hypnotizing me with those beautiful brown innocent eyes.

"W " H i l

"I will." He said

He wiped my nut from the corner of his mouth and drove off. I went back inside
and straightened the house back up, waiting for my wife to get home…

Alisha

...ome around midnight, because I get off work at 11:00pm---well, that's just what ...
...sband, I really get off at 8:00pm. But telling my husband 11:00 gives me more ti...
...ith Ebony. When I got in scented candles were lit and Latrell was on the couch sl...
...cefully. I walked over to him and stared at the gorgeous man in front of me. He ...
...chocolate mocha complected man with a million-dollar smile and honey hazel eye...
...e so thick, juicy and soft. His body was exquisite; the gym was a second home for...
...fingers through his long, wavy hair and squeezed his muscle bound arms. I ador...
...n I was married to, he just didn't have what I wanted at times---and that was a pus...

My nail accidentally scratched his scalp and he jumped up in fear. He
smiled and lowered his guard when he realized it was just me.

"Oh what's up baby? You scared me. " He said
Wiping sleep away from his eyes.

"I'm fine, sorry I woke you. Why are you so tired?" I asked.

"Long day, hardly got any sleep last night." He replied

"Okay well just go ahead and go back to sleep baby, I got to get my
shit ready for work tomorrow anyway so you can---."

He shut me up by pressing his thick lips against mine. He held my cheeks as our
...ongues danced with each other. My arms wrapped around his neck and he slappe...
...y apple behind. He was still damp, probably from a shower, with him rubbing al...
...er me all it did was get *me* damp. He nibbled my neck and I dropped my purse ar...
...keys where I stood as he knelt, and licked me from the belly button on down…

Latrell

ny way to her pelvis and snatched away her pants, removing her panties slowly like
. Sex with my woman was common only because I made it that way. I didn't want
hip to decrease just because I was being freaky on the side. So I just gave her the d
suspect anything. I licked around her pussy lips, letting my tongue explore my terr
ingers through my damp hair, combing my mane gently. I got up and lifted her sh
watching her breasts bounce slightly. Those succulent dark nipples were erect and
upon. I laid her down on the floor and began bathing her entire body with my to
wet and screaming for me to enter, so I let my dick free from my boxers and slid d

Alisha

t pained me to know that he just got through eating a pussy that a female just got
through enjoying not even an hour ago. But I couldn't tell him, it would hurt him
even more if I told him he was swapping spit with some other woman. He pressed
inside putting all his length and girth in my pussy. I moaned instantly.

Sex with Latrell was amazing; he knew every spot on my body that made
me scream, and every spot that sent chills down my spine.

"Oh shit." I said

funny how when you're getting some good dick the only thing you can think of t
y is a curse word. But then again, a few 'damn daddy's' and a couple of 'oooh fucl
at pussy' phrases makes it better all the more. He was very aggressive in bed and
d it. I gripped his back and sunk my nails deep into his flesh as he dug deep into
tight hole. I worked my pussy muscles to make him moan and speak gibberish.

"Damn girl, you make this dick feel good." He said
"You like this pussy?" I responded
"HELL YEAH"
"What?" I said, pretending I didn't hear him
"HELL YEAH!"
"I can't hear you daddy!"
"Hell motha fuckin yeah!"

ncreased his speed and tore my insides up, causing me to scream his name. He ye
at the top of his lungs and decorated my breasts and neck with his nut. He slipp
self back inside and rested on top of me, dick still throbbing like a steady heartbe

"You were amazing." I said
"Likewise."

always made sure I let him know how good he was in bed, so he wouldn't begin to
hink that I was losing interest in him sexually. He was good don't get me wrong,
he was damn good. However, I didn't want any suspicions to rise. It had been a

Latrell

p on the floor next to my wife and analyzed the fine woman that I became one wi
green eyes and slim waist. She had a high fat booty that was toned and perfectly
all waist that was perfect to grab when I hit it from the back. Down to those slen
inine feet. She had her tongue pierced and chin as well. She got hers the same ti
brow pierced. I stood up and carried her to the bed. She looked exhausted so I t
f contacting her job and called in sick for her. I on the other hand had to go to w
d, dressed, and headed out. Traffic was ridiculous in Las Vegas, plenty of accident
n the Veg think they are the 'King of the Road' until they hit somebody and beco
oad Kill'. I drove down Craig rd. to Clayton and parked at the 24-Hour Fitness.
nal trainer/fitness instructor. My classes ranged from 1-3 hour sessions with abou
ay I worked. My first class didn't start for some time so I decided to kill time by
self before my class started. I grabbed two 40lb. Weights and started some curls.
nd the room at all the men—not in a freaky kind of way—just their facial express

re were the ones with the serious faces that came to the gym to work out and not
nds, then the steroid popping body builders who overworked themselves to the p
exhaustion, only to satisfy their definition of perfection. It was sad, but unfortun
it was what the world came to, a world full of imperfection, striving for perfectior
into my workspace and got prepared as my students started to pour in. I waited
eir stretches, building cardio before we began. I was waiting for Darius who was
y wait wasn't in vain when his sexy ass walked in; I admired him in many ways tha
l" about 170 or 175, slim but far from skinny—thick in all the right places. He h
ir and a blinding smile. His Mississippi accent turned me on all the more. He sa
d got in his place all the way up front, by me of course. He flashed me a look and
re his head. Darius always worked out with his shirt off, which was no problem fo
s banging' and he showed it off proudly. I licked my lips and began my instructic
s to bend down and begin the toe touches. I patrolled around the room, and then
eir way to Darius' high, fat booty to his thick muscular calves. I blinked out of t
me in and turned the radio on. I placed Missy Elliot's CD *The Cookbook* in an
ntrol' on repeat. My theory was that good music always hyped someone up for a

were our pushups, then mountain climbers, and right to our curls with the free w
"That's it people!" I encouraged
ow sweat was glistening on all of our bodies and we were actually only halfway th

e day. I smirked at the exhausted group, passed out on the floor catching their bre

"Good workout." Darius said, wiping sweat from his forehead.
"That's my job." I said, undressing his sexy frame, looking him up & down.

started packing my stuff as the people walked out waving goodbye and saying thei
ank you's. Everyone had left and I was ready to leave myself. I turned and bumpe
to Darius who was sneakily behind me the whole time. He grabbed my dick and
squeezed unmercifully. My mouth instantly opened preparing to moan.

"Shhh." He said.
Placing his finger over my lips, stopping my moan in it's' tracks.
"You worked me out pretty good today." He whispered in my ear.

"Now it's time for me to give you a workout of my own."
ed my bags when he placed his lips around my dick, already hard from his grip. I
lick all around the head of my dick, collecting my pre-come. I placed my hands
f his head making him engulf the entire shaft of my dick. He held my balls and p
em while I moaned and massaged his scalp. I opened my eyes and realized I was
o one was in the room with us but I was never the type of person to take risky ch

"What's wrong?" Darius asked after I snatched my dick out of his mouth.
"Not here." I said "Come by later while Alisha is still at work."
"As always." He said rolling his eyes.
"What the fuck does that mean?" I asked
"You always have to mix Alisha in with our business, it gets tiring sometimes."
"She's my wife nigga, what did you expect?"
"Then why are you with me instead of her every night?" he asked

dn't like the fact that he put me on complete hush-mode but he did have a very va
. Yes I am fucking some dude while my wedding wing still rests on my finger, bu
he stipulations of our relationship from jump, so I was at fault of nothing in my e
ted my semi-hard dick inside my pants, got my belongings, and headed for the do

"Wait baby, im sorry!" he yelled at me as I proceeded to walk out.

sat in my car and turned on the radio, Bow Wow and Ciara were playing through
y ears while my guilt and shame raced through my mind. I wasn't cool with what
was doing, but my conscience wasn't strong enough to make me stop. I took out
my dick and jacked off, releasing the built up stress on my steering wheel.

en though my husband called in for me I decided to go anyway. If I didn't go to w
en my alibi for coming home so late would no longer be valid, Ebony was my sou
extreme pleasure, whenever I had the opportunity to get it I would, so missing wo
was not an option. Nevertheless, I wasn't going to deny the fact that I was tired.
a going to lunch Jane." I said, poking my head in my supervisor's office on my way
e door. My next destination was Starbucks. I got my usual Venti Mocha-Frapucci
with whipped cream and chocolate drizzle on the top. After getting my cup of wak
I decided to spend the remainder of my lunch break with Ebony so I made my w
towards the Nellis Air Force base to Eagle Traces, Ebony's apartment complex.

"What's up sweet heart?" Ebony said
I walked inside and gave her a kiss. Making my insides shake.
"I've missed you, what have you been up to?" she asked

Her teasing was amusing, and it damn sure was working. She was walking around
in tube socks and a T-shirt that was obviously too big for her. Her breasts, so
perky and alive, made the shirt stick out farther than it was designed to.

"Nothing, you know me—just doin' my thing."
"Apparently not with me since I haven't heard from you all day."
"First of all, I was just here last night, and secondly, I was working, you
know *some* people do that instead of stay at home all damn day."

felt a headache approaching. She got less and less attractive once my anger began
se with her. She knew I had a commitment with my husband…well, somewhat o
ommitment. But I explained this to her thoroughly prior to us beginning this fli
"Ebony, why are you trippin?"
"I'm trippin' because every time I here you say you are *'doing your
thing'* I know that *'thing'* includes your husband."

ny coffee on the table and walked towards her. I played with my tongue ring and
the eye. There was hurt and emptiness in her soul. With each blink she held bac
ars that I was the cause of. I didn't like what I was doing to her, I would come ov

"Thou shall not commit adultery."

"I'm so sorry."
Was all I could say to her, I knew it didn't really help her situation
but my apologies, and remorse was all I could offer.

married Latrell I loved him to death and still do, never did I suspect that I would
like this. I married him out of love and I would never leave him for someone else,
. I vowed to never tell him at all and I planned to keep the covenant I placed upor
re to ever slip up and he found out, the consequences would be more than catacly
d her cheek with the back of my hand and gave her the biggest hug I could muste
e down into tears telling me she didn't mean what she said and hoped I could forg
I just squeezed tighter, my grandmother used to tell me that sometimes a good h
a good cry could do more for a person than any words that you could possibly say.
held her until she let out all of her stored emotions. About ten minutes later she
the bathroom to gather herself, mumbling unnecessary apologies as she walked. N
n began to take over, watching each of her butt cheeks bounce with her every step
"Oh my God." I whispered to myself
I grabbed my cell phone and punched in my supervisor's number.
"Traffic is a bitch; I'm going to be a little late coming back."
ying became a second nature to me; it was now to the point where my lies became
involuntary, spewing from my mouth without even thinking about it.

e lioness was on the prowl, I walked towards her…gazed at her in front of the sinl
ing tissue under her eyes to capture her tears. I got directly behind her and locked
eyes with her brown beauties; if I had a dick it would have been erect, poking he
ack. My fingers caressed her oblique's, danced over her pussy, thanking God for let
ecide not to wear panties today. One by one my fingers began to enter her, nibbl
biting on her neck, holding her in place as I watched her squirm in the mirror.

her around, her back now on the wall, our tongues greeted each other with a pas
ught I could only feel for my husband. Piece by piece our clothes began to disapp
until we were left with nothing but what we were brought into this world with.

"Do a handstand." I ordered
Her face oozed of confusion and excitement
"What?" she asked, panting, breathing uneven
"Do a fucking handstand." I spoke

With her in this vulnerable state of mind, this was the perfect opportunity
to allow my freak to roam free, bending her to my will.
Hesitantly, but surely, she did as she was told. resting on the wall with her back
keeping balance. Her beautiful feet now within my view, among other things.

"Spread em'." I demanded once more

This time with no argument her legs spread in the air, making a perfect V shape

I dined, engulfed her pussy in my mouth as I gyrated my hips,
marinating her mouth with my own juices.
the same three fingers in as before, mimicking the in and out motions of a dick, h
shake, I slapped them loud and hard, making them steady as I ate and stroked he
uch blood to the head can kill a human being, so I knew I had to make her come
Faster, faster my fingers stroked inside, her moaning growing stronger, her
pitch switching from alto to soprano. I knew she was close.
I rested her thighs on my shoulders as she continued to lick me,
scream out my name as I buried my face even deeper.
1, 2, 3 squirts blasted into my face…blinding me temporarily in one eye.

I laid her down gently on the floor, her trembling and satisfied body
regaining the blood that had rushed to her cranium.
I wiped my face, licked off whatever residue was on my hands and lips, then
went to her and laid by her side, looking her right in the eye. More tears, I
thought it was my come on her face but those were all her tears.

"I love you Alisha, I love you."
I caressed her face and smiled, knowing in my heart that returning the love
was impossible…she did not have my heart, she only had my pussy.
"I know." I said.

-applying myself I grabbed my coffee and went back to work. Ebony called me or
vas driving, telling me how sorry she was for overreacting earlier. I giggled and let
apology was accepted, and she could show me how much more sorry she was whe
h after work. I clicked my phone off, somewhat sorry for Ebony yet still concerne
nd my own situation. I wasn't afraid of getting caught, just cautious. Going back
:n two lovers and not giving a damn who it was hurting in the process was risky. I
:ave the game someday I hoped. Latrell hasn't suspected nor has he asked me any
ing my whereabouts and I didn't plan on letting him know anything either so I m:
thing on a "don't ask, don't tell basis. I got to my job and saw a bouquet of roses
ard that said *because you deserve them* with Latrells' neatly written signature on the

I smelled the cards scent that was covered in Latrells' sweet smelling cologne. A
tear and a smile decorated my face as a co-worker shouted

should start being the good woman to Latrell that I knew I could be.

"Jane, I'm sorry but I'm just not feeling well—I need to get out of here." I said clenching my stomach, making my lie a tad bit more believable.

I got in my car and raced back to Ebony's house…

Latrell

...ome and checked my messages to find 2 of them from Darius. I reminded myself...
...once I saw him later on. He knew damn well that calling my home was strictly fc...
...eeded was for my wife to come home and check the messages before I did and tha...
...en it, my life and everything I had invested into it would have been done for. The...
...ever wanted to do was hurt Alisha, and since I knew that telling her about my dir...
...r, I decided it was best to keep it to myself. I at down on my couch and flipped on...
...atched Student Center on BET. It always concerned me that African Americans ol...
...nat represented the community as a whole, besides UPN but that didn't count sinc...
...ows weren't worth watching. In my opinion ever since The Parkers was cancelled, '...
...I.V. any more. I tried the best I could to suppress my anger for Darius until he ca...
...ut it overflowed and before I knew it my finger was pressing 'send' on my cell pho...

"What's up daddy?" he answered
"What the fuck did I tell you?" I screamed.
"About what?"
"Don't play dumb."
"Oh." He said
"Oh?" I spoke confused "That's all you got to say?"

"I meant sorry, I must have dialed the wrong number."
"How the fuck do you dial the wrong number five times in a row?"
"I said I was sorry!" he snapped

I heard him let out a puff of air and he spoke again
"I guess I forgot that your precious wife meant more to you than me."

...damn right she does! Now I ain't finna start this shit with your ass today!" I excl...

He chuckled

...nny, because you sure do like to finish with this ass every night before your wife g...
...I damn near dropped the phone at his comment. I told him to call me before he...
...ame through as always so we could finish our conversation in person. I didn't kn...
...why I always clammed up when he brought my wife into our affairs. I suppose m...
guilt clashed with my pleasure which caused a total internal shutdown.

rows we shared and the kiss that sealed the deal. Then to our honey moon; we wer

nd made love on the beach while the tide covered our bodies, and the warm sand i

inner fires. Then the freakiness inside surfaced and we skipped the love making, a

l all up, down, and through that hotel room. We should have been fined for how

we left on the sheets. I jumped to the sound of my cell phone ringing and answer

"Hello?" I answered groggily
"Sup baby?" Alisha asked
"Nothing' much, what's up?"

cking on my husband, making sure all was fine, and to also let him know that I mi

"Well that is awfully sweet of you, but you know you aren't
allowed to be making personal calls at work."

h you're right, but love wouldn't be love if risks weren't taken now would it?" she s

"Hmm, I guess you're right." I answered "I love you."
"Love you too—see you after work."

and wiped my eyes to hear my phone go off again, this time it was Darius on the

"Are you ready" he said as soon as I answered
"Yeah, let me get in the shower and I'll be ready."
"Okay, I'm on my way." He said
"Alright, I'll be waiting."
"I should be there in 10, I love---."

ckly hung up the phone before he could finish dropping the approaching 'L' boml

hat blamed myself for it. I stuck strictly on pleasure while his growing feelings we

ed, or better yet, not acknowledged in the least. However, he had a choice, I expla

at the circumstances were, and it wasn't not my fault he did not want to adhere to

and saw my shorts sticky and wet from my dream of me and my wife's' honeymoo

l and made myself more presentable for Darius, as soon as I finished brushing my

doorbell ring. My dick instantly rose to attention, and the adrenaline began to r

to do my thing that I did so well, and the fact that I was already angry at Darius

s ass was going to receive all of my built up emotion. He won't walk right for a we

Alisha

aid in her bed smoking the remainder of the cush blunt we were sharing. I inhale
rge portion and trapped it in my mouth. I then leaned toward Ebony and kissed h
ntly; transferring the smoke into her moth. She exhaled the smoke out of her mo
and nose over my chest and nipples, its warmth causing my body to tingle.

"You're nasty." Ebony said with a smile
"You say nasty, I say experienced." I responded

iggled and laid next to each other watching the smoke rise into the air and shift it
d the room. Ebony turned to her side and watched me inhale & exhale with skill
gh. I caught her staring harder than normal; I knew something had to be on her n

"Why are you looking at me like that?" I asked smirking.
"You'll get mad if I told you."

didn't like how she said that. Whenever she let me know I would get mad before s
told me, our conversation usually would get sour and indeed leave me highly upse
I leaned up in the bed preparing for a serious conversation.
"What." I said rolling my eyes.
She took a deep breath and sighed.

was talking to my brother today about our situation, he completely understood wl
was coming from, he told me he dealt with the same predicament once before. Ar
he's my older brother so I really look up to him and respect his opinion so--."

"Ebony!" I yelled, aggravated with her obvious stalling
"Long story short, I think it's best if you and Latrell got a divorce."

I put the blunt in the ashtray and got off the bed.
"Where are you going?" she asked
"I'm leaving." I said grabbing my clothes and other belongings.
"What's wrong?" she said putting on her panties.
"Why the fuck do you say shit like that?" I asked

"You are the last bitch to be talking about honesty."

ed what I was doing and stared at her. She walked past me, brushing my shoulder
er way to the living room. The left half of my brain told me to snatch the bitch up
or calling me out of my name, the logical part of my brain told me to shake it off,
me wouldn't make it in jail for killing this chick. I walked towards the door and t
looked back at Ebony and shook my head. She sat on the couch flipping the chai
vision as If I had disappeared. I left and slammed the door behind me, I heard son
d crash but at that moment I didn't give a fuck. She disrespected me tonight and i
vas uncalled for. I was driving on my way home when my cell rang. It was Ebony,
l ignore and went on about my business. About 5 minutes from pulling up to my l

Latrell

I was getting some head from Darius when I heard the garage go up.

"Oh shit." I said

ickly got up, picked up as much of his stuff as possible and raced out the door butt

n as he closed the front door behind him Alisha came through the back from the g

'What's up sweetheart?" I said, wearing the fakest smile in the history of counterfei

She looked pissed and smelled like fresh weed. She gave me a short but less
than convincing smirk and dashed her way to the bedroom and shut the
door. I let out a huge breath of relief and laid flat on the couch.
That was too fucking close…

Alisha

house smelled of latex and body heat when I walked into my home, but my high ɛ
lingering headache I had made me not pay it too much attention. I got naked once
the bedroom and laid stomach first on the bed, in tears. By the time I was through
was covered in snot, spit and drool. I don't know why I cried so much but it was
started, I just couldn't stop. All of my fears and pain just poured out of me in the
y streams running down my face. My granny always did say that it was better to
n keep it in. I sat up sniffing and walked into the bathroom that was connected t
er bedroom me and Latrell shared, I had to take a piss. As I sat down and took a ʋ
xing pee, I glanced over to the bathtub and saw some underwear lying on the floc
But they sure didn't look like my husbands'.

Latrell

: the first 3 hours she was locked up in the room I started to get a little worried. I ¦
stayed awake just to make sure everything was alright with her. Lord knows that I ¦
shit myself when she got home earlier than expected. Poor Darius, I made a menta¦
e him a call later and apologize. I was just about to go to the kitchen and get som¦
when I heard a buzzing sound. I looked around and saw Alisha's cell phone vibrati¦
ng up in her purse. She must have been so angry that she dropped all her stuff whe¦
in. I wasn't quick enough to answer it so by the time I got to it the screen flashed '¦
I checked to see who it was so I could let her know to give a call to whoever it was¦

ut to no avail, the number was restricted. I put her phone back inside her purse a¦
it on the counter then went back to my business. I was putting some oil in the sk¦
n I heard the buzzing again. This time it was a text message from her mom. I nor¦
ouldn't snoop, but it could have been important, so I clicked on the message. It re¦

> *'Sorry sweetie, I know I have been getting on your bad side lately and I do*
> *apologize. Promise me that you will call me so we can talk? Love you…'*

I heard the handle on the bedroom jiggle so I quickly placed her phone back in he¦
purse as if it never had been touched, and continued preparing my meal.

Alisha

ked in the kitchen to see Latrell putting some chicken on the stove. Then I looked
nd saw my purse on the counter, when I know I left it on the floor when I came in

it." I whispered to myself after realizing I didn't take my cell phone with me. The
me and my lover was in the same room with Latrell for more than 4 hours that m
omfortable. I swallowed some spit and put a fake smile on my face and greeted my

"Hey baby." I said, rubbing his chest.
ng, how you feeling sleepy head?" he asked. Not taking his eyes from the popping

I walked to the refrigerator and grabbed myself a Dr. Pepper.
"I'm better now." I lied

ent I was better but my life still wasn't what I always dreamt it would be. I quickly
e and walked back to the bedroom and locked the door. I turned my purse upside
s contents onto the floor, and then out dropped my cell. I flipped it open and sav
as an already read text message from my mom. I thanked God once more for gra
e, a while back a played a scenario in my head. Asking myself that if Latrell ever g
at would my alibi be? So I took it upon myself to save Ebony's number under 'Mc
questions. My mother died of a cocaine overdose when I was ten, may Lucifer rest
't know much about her, my granny never felt comfortable going into details abou
aughter. So I left it alone, and now the mother I never knew became my scapegoat

none away from me after reading the message. It was stopped in its' tracks by the
erwear I noticed earlier. I picked up my belongings and placed them back inside
th the drawers and cell phone. I wasn't sure if Latrell had already seen the message
I'd be damned if I was the only one to be made a fool if push came to shove. Afte
my purse I walked back into the bedroom to find Latrell in the bed, out like a lig
overed in ranch and hot sauce to the kitchen and washed it, along with the other
was late, Lord knows I was tired but couldn't sleep. After making sure my husban
I analyzed the strange undergarments. They were fresh silk, a 32 in the waist, my
Whoever they belonged to had to be on the petite side. They weren't cheap; who
sure had style. I weighed my options; maybe he switched underwear without tell

o him and stared him up and down; he was lying on his back, dick hard and stiff.
climbed on top of him, gyrated my hips as he slowly awakened. I sat on his dick,
descending slowly, as my pussy stretched to the contours of his member.

roke up and grabbed my waist, entering himself deeper inside. I bounced up and
ng my breasts and licking my nipples. I moaned, scratched, yelled, hollered and sc
ism as I felt him release his warm prize inside of me. I laid on my mans' chest and
n a deep sleep, mentally slapping myself for ever thinking that this man of mine w
on me, that thought was completely unreal to me. I felt so dumbfounded that I le
ight like that even enter my mind. My pussy was way too good for him to go astra

Latrell

e while that Alisha was in the living room I was awake. Darius had texted me not
sked if I had seen his underwear that he left in the bathroom. When I searched an
em, the only logical explanation would have been that my wife was sitting on the
y smelling the underwear she found. I knew my woman like the back of my hand.
hought I did until that odd text message from her mother, the mother that I neve
My ego convinced me that there was absolutely no way that she could be cheatin
after the way I be layin' the pipe, she knew better than to go searching for any ne

Latrell

woke up alone, and rested. It was my off day but Alisha had to go in which was ve
inconvenient at times. Our schedules collided with each other, and because of that v
er got a chance to sit at home and cuddle or hold each other after we made love, th
t I've always wanted to do with her. I craved the emotional benefits of a relationsh
as the spiritual and physical. My emotions were built up deep, deep inside and we
being let out. It bothered me but nevertheless, I had my ways of dealing with it.

"Did you get caught?" Darius asked

I called him about an hour or so after I woke up since I didn't get a chance to get in
touch with him the night before after coming so close to being caught in the act.

"No, she was cool. Something else was bothering her though."
"Like what?" he asked
"I don't know, probably her cycle." I said
"Yeah, 'TOM' can be a real bitch sometimes." He responded
"Who is Tom?" I asked confused
"You know, T.O.M. as in 'Time of the Month'..."

I giggled at his cute analogy and turned on the radio.
"So what's on your schedule for today?" I asked with KeKe Wyatt and
Avants' 'Nothing in This World' filling the living room.

"Nothing that I know of, just chill at the house I guess."
"That's not the answer I was looking for." I said
"Well then correct my error Mr. Daniels."
"You were supposed to say that you will be here in 15 minutes to finish sucking th
nut out of my dick and hug you until we fall asleep," I said all in one breath
"I'll be there in 8."

sure I showered and made myself presentable for my lover. To be honest, I didn't
ng more than to stop fucking with Darius altogether but I just couldn't stop. Ever
t got busted I had a feeling in my gut telling me that she could come in through th
instead of the garage. But there was no time to think about the pros and cons, I'v

ime I turned around he was naked, dick hanging like an ornament. I grabbed his
d pulled him closer to me, locking our lips in an unbreakable embrace. Our hard
d with each time our tongues greeted. I held his manhood and gripped tightly as i
ue even deeper, kissing me harder, making him moan as if he was already getting f
ed him up by his ass as he wrapped his sexy muscular legs around my wais. He m
nd down the shaft of my hard dick still in my shorts, the friction making me harc

"Latrell!!" Alisha's' voice yelled.

I dropped Darius where we stood and looked around.
No one…no one was here but me and Darius.
he fuck is your problem?!?" Darius asked, rising from the floor, breathing uncontr
"Did you hear that?" I asked
"Hear what?" He asked, my paranoia becoming contagious,
spreading to him as he nervously looked around.

ny head and rubbed my eyes. For years my conscience had been suppress and now
wanted to make its' appearance. I took a deep breath and studied the man in fror

"Never mind." I said as I took his hand and led him to the bedroom.
"You sure you are okay baby?" he asked

I took off my shorts and dropped them to the floor.

"Bend over nigga." I said. Gripping my dick in hand

I turned him over and watched him touch his toes, I listened as he moaned
and squirmed when I placed my throbbing dick inside.

"Damn, that's what I'm talkin' about." I said

I fucked him like no other, listening to his moans, replacing
them with the voices I was hearing in my head…

Alisha

ork feeling refreshed and revived, walking with great pride in myself. My co-work
me any shit and my boss had been giving me compliments all day long. Towards
lay I left my desk to use the bathroom. Which wasn't a good time but my bladder
the liquid. At this time of the day stuck up females would crowd the bathroom bei
ssiping about other people without recognizing their own problems; typical messy

I washed my hands and headed back to my desk. When I walked in the office
I saw a large group of about five or six people hovering over my desk.

"What's going on?" I asked

ey all jumped at the sound of my voice, turned around, somewhat shielding my de

l like to sit down now." I said, pointing to them surrounding my chair. They scatt
xplace like a cockroach to a light switch. I shook my head and searched my desk,
iosity for what they were looking at. They were simply beautiful, two dozen beau
that smelled like heaven on a stem. They were on my desk without a care in the v

"They must be from Latrell." I spoke to myself as I searched for a card. My
eyes watered as I lifted the card from its' petite envelope.

"Because you deserve it."

I didn't realize how much I had cried until I looked at my shirt covered in
teardrops. I wiped my eyes and raced to the phone, dialing up Latrell.

"Hello." He said
"I love you so much." I said still crying my heart out
"For what?" he asked
t be modest, the flowers silly! Thank you, and not just for the flowers, but for eve
else too, you are such a good man and I adore you. Do you trust that I love you?
"Of course I do." He responded.
"I will call you when I get off work love."
"Alright, I'm not going anywhere."

"Damn, who put poison in your coffee today?" she joked.

I'm sorry; I just think that my baby might be suspecting something."

"Why would I suspect anything?" she asked

"I was referring to Latrell."

"Oh."

ed and loving voice she had in the beginning of our conversation disappeared. I c
dn't appreciate how I was running my game but it wasn't any of my concern, she k
m the beginning, and she knew this is what she signed up for when she read the fi

"So are we kickin' it tonight or are you and your baby going to be busy?"

"I think I will spend some time with Latrell today; give him a massage or something, just to let him know I still care, you know how it is." I said

know. Tend to him temporarily then come to my house and eat my pussy." She s:

"What?" I spoke, my pitch rising

"Don't trip; call me when you pull my number."

about to call that bitch back and cuss her out for hanging up on me but I was sti
rk and I had a certain level of professionalism I had to uphold. Besides, I was stil
high off of the gift my husband gave to me. I took a single rose from the bouquet and sniffed it, basking in the glorious fragrance…

Latrell

sure what Alisha was talking about when she mentioned flowers, but I played along
ire who sent her flowers but it sure wasn't me. It sounded like something I would
't do it. This really made me wonder what the fuck was going on. First that rando
: from the mother I've never heard about, and now flowers sent from an unknown

I called Darius to see what was up with him.
"So where have you been?" Darius asked
"Nowhere, why you ask that?"
[ell, you haven't called me to finish our conversation about the run in with your w:
"Oh yeah, about that…are you okay?" I said, giving off a slight chuckle

"Oh so you think that shit was funny?" He asked
"Actually, it was a little bit, you run kind of fast."

"Oh I guess I missed the joke about me running out of your house
in my birthday suit, my bad." He said sarcastically
"Come on man, have a fucking sense of humor." I said
"Ha-ha hell." He said hanging up in my face

ok stuff way too seriously; I was just playing with him. I called back about two o
ire times and got nothing but his voicemail. He would call back, that was for cert

I sat down and watched television for the remainder of my day.

tfall came as fast as it could have possibly come that day; I'm sure daylights' saving
some part to play in it. My nights were lonely to due Alisha's work schedule. Tha
of the main reasons that fueled me to seek attention from Darius. At first my inte
only experimental, just to try it out. But I made myself into a lie once I did it the
    The next thing I knew I grew accustomed to it and ended up enlarging what I th
s going to be only a one-night stand. When I thought about it, Darius had somev
there for me since day one. We went to high school together, both graduates of C
gs High School at the top of our class. He was even at my wedding, smiling right
knowing I had just ate him out the night before. Out of all my fears the only one
f the list was hurting my wife. The bible speaks clearly about how things that are

y didn't accept any unplanned visits but I was stressed and my dick was already ha
an exception. He got to my house about 15 minutes after hanging up with me, lo
ual. Before I could express my apologies for joking with him earlier he was already
, doing what he did best. Once again letting me know just how damn good sin fe

Alisha

way home I thought about what my life would have been like without Ebony by m
ly wouldn't be stressed, my headaches wouldn't be as frequent, and I also wouldn't b
amount of pleasure I got from her. Latrell didn't know I was coming home; I want
rise to thank him for the gift he gave earlier. We never got to spend any real time t
ait to see the look on his face when I walk in and tell him I came home, just to be v

Latrell

As I had Darius screaming my name, the voices continued to ring in my head. The last thing I wanted was for my wife to make a trip home.

Alisha

What is a surprise if you give clues to your arrival? So I didn't go through the garage, instead I just parked out front and made my way to the front door.

Latrell

Damn.

is ran into my bedroom and hid in the closet as soon as we heard the doorknob jig

Alisha

I put my key in the door…

Latrell

She turned the doorknob…

Alisha

I opened the door and walked inside to see my husband on the couch watching television with a blanket covering the lower half of his body.

'What's up baby?" he said as I closed the door
Nothing, why is it so stuffy up in here? Were you working out or something?" I ask

"Yeah, something like that. A few push-ups and crunches." He said

ffed around my home, that damn smell again. It was giving me a headache, but I s off, picking an unnecessary fight wasn't my intention for skipping a night with Ebo

'I was thinking we spend some more time together—get some movies and chill lik the old days, before our schedules started conflicting." I said, sitting on his lap.

"Sounds cool, thanks for surprising me." He said
"So my surprise was a success?" I asked

He looked at me and smiled so hard I thought his cheeks were going to burst.

"More than you know." He spoke
"I'm going to go get out of my work clothes and run to Blockbuster, you go and make us some snacks and open up that new Alize' I just bought okay?" I said

Making my way to the closet to make my appearance a little bit more decent than what I was wearing, rocking the 'hard day at work' look wasn't my style.

7ait!" Latrell yelled, dropping his blanket to the floor exposing his heavy equipmen

Latrell

My naked body was the least of my worries. If I hadn't stopped her she would have undoubtedly spotted Darius hiding his naked frame behind our wardrobes.

d just hop in the shower first, and then get dressed." I said, moving her into our t

ou're right; I'm not smelling too hot anyway." She said, making a funny face to d or from a long days' work. When the only thing I smelled was my fear, seeping th s. She went into the restroom and shut the door behind her. I let out the biggest ef and rushed Darius out of the house—naked again—but I didn't have time to w

"What are you taking your sweet little time for, hurry up and get the fuck out!" I hispered as soft as I possibly could, and yet loud enough so he could get my point

"I'm gonna leave nigga, wait a minute!"

Darius continued to move slowly, seemingly on purpose just to irritate me, torturing me in my time of vulnerability.

later." He said, smirking as he walked out of my door. I was pissed beyond desc arius and the childish games he would play to jeopardize my marriage. But I coul v any emotion out of the ordinary in order to keep the suspicion level at its lowest lack woman has a very keen eye for change; especially when it comes to her man.

I heard the bathroom door open and I immediately followed the sound.

"That was refreshing." She said, drying off her soaking wet body.

icked my lips and stared as the towel traveled across her delicate curves and plum s. My dick rose to attention and all thought of Darius was gone. She got dressed nd gave me a kiss before she left to pick up the movies. I put on some boxers and hed my home from top to bottom—no pun intended. I found a few drips of co

I jumped at the sound of knocking on my patio door; the only way to get back there was with a key to the gate, or awesome jumping skills to get over that wall. So whoever it was, was obviously not an invited guest.

I grabbed my 3-80 secretly tucked under my couch and slowly walked toward the sound. I opened the door quickly and pointed my gun at the first body I saw.

"Wait! Don't shoot!" A female voice screamed.

She held up her hands in surrender as the tip of my gun stared at her cranium.

"Who the fuck are you?" I asked, clutching the cold steel in hands. Her eyes traveled from the hard bulge in my pants, to the gun, then back to my eyes.

"I'm looking for Alisa, is she here?" she asked.

ler eyes…full of so much emotion. It was only for a moment but when I locked e ith her, I could feel that her heart was in deep pain, it was like I recognized those e efore. It was like I was looking into Darius' eyes, eyes that expose ones inner feelir of wanting to be loved, the desire to be held and cared for, for the rest of your life

I lowered my gun and let her in, sobbing, her body shaking uncontrollably.

"I apologize for coming in this way; I'm a friend of Alisha's'."
"So why haven't I met you before?" I asked, keeping the gun within her view.

"Well we kind of had a big argument the last time we chilled, so I'm not surprised that she hasn't mentioned me before."

itling her as being beautiful would be an insult, this girl was downright fine. I sto ere in my trance, still stressed and full of anger from the turn of events that had ta ace today. Apart of me wanted to call off our night for quality time, I don't like to ered while my emotions are on the rise. Because my flesh, always clouded my judg ausing me to do things that I never would normally do if my emotions were stab

I ended the staring competition I was having with her breasts and focused my attention back to those ridiculously familiar eyes.
I clicked the safety back on and put it back in its original spot. I walked over

"But you don't even know my name." she said
"I didn't ask."

it for her until she gets back?" she asked "Please, she's the best thing to ever happe

y head, embarrassed at how powerless I became when it came to a beautiful woma

"Yeah, aiight." I said, walking back into the bedroom to grab a
t-shirt "You sure you want to wait for her?" I asked
"Yeah its fine, I'm used to being a second priority."

as soon as she formed the words in her brain the tears began to stream down her
deep and like none other that I had ever seen. I walked towards her as fast as I cou
t. Her body was so warm, skin so smooth and smelled of fresh cocoa butter. Ou
once more, and before I knew it our lips met. My anger and frustration instantan
peared, along with her shirt, as my boxers were yanked down to the floor. I turned
and nibbled all along her earlobe and neck as she held my earlobe captive in her n

off the lights and laid her down onto the floor, I knew that my wife could be hom
But my stress level was too high, and my dick was too hard for my brain to distin
right and wrong. I forced my dick inside of her as my sweat dripped onto her bro
like I had never moaned before as her pussy contracted and compressed on my d
utes ago I was preparing to end my sin, live out the remainder of my life with my
is sin had an orgasm creating hold on me and I was gripping onto it tighter every

Alisha

It was Friday so Blockbuster was semi-crowded with people walking around,
not really   knowing what they wanted to get but still enjoyed the pleasure of lookir
I looked at my cell phone and saw I had no missed calls, or text messages from
Ebony, that was not a usual thing for me.

There wasn't a day that went by where Ebony didn't at least send a text message.
her house phone and got no answer. I didn't know why but I felt a slight trickle o

I grabbed the closest movie to me and headed straight for Ebony's house…

Latrell

"Oh Shit!" I screamed as I shot my kids all on her face and chest.

"Damn daddy." She said, biting down on her bottom lip.

nd got a towel for her and myself, after washing up I went into my bedroom and c
door behind me and locking it. Before laying down I went back
living room.

"She'll be here in a lil' bit alright?"
oking at her tears rolling down her face. I didn't feel bad for what I did at first, I n
was frustrated and needed to let some emotion out, she just happe
there.
Damn, what was her name?

Alisha

"Ebony!!"
I screamed as I violently banged on her front door. I knew Ebony all to
to know that she was up to something, something crazy. That bitch wa
as hell and revenge was her middle name. I quickly got back in my ca
floored it all the way to my house. My hands were shaking of anxiety , I
the wheel as tight as I could, luckily making it home with no injuri

Latrell

my bed, relieved, exhausted, and guilty. For once I felt like I did something wror
as always I swatted away my guilt like a mosquito and turned on the ᵀ

I heard the front door as Alisha's key turned the lock…

Alisha

I unlocked the door....

Latrell

The squeaky doorknob I had been meaning to get fixed turned....

Alisha

I opened the door…

…eyes lost their sweet color as I saw that bitch sitting on my couch eating chips, wat…
Madeas' Family Reunion.

"Hey baby, what's up?" she said
"What the fuck are you doing at my house?" I asked
"Just chillin, waiting for you."

"Where is Latrell?"
…He's in the room, so that is the famous Latrell huh? He is too fine, now I see why y…
like to spend more time with him than me, I aint mad at you girl…

…ll the strength I had left within my body to keep me from hitting her straight in th…
mouth. So I placed my stuff on the coffee table and went into my bed…

…by." Latrell said as I walked in "Who is your friend? She came over here earlier for…
you were out; she wanted to wait for you so I figured it was something in…

…weet babe, but that's just my old friend from high school, she just got in town and…
old road dog to hang with her, you know how it is. I said, lying through…

…nted to be angry, had every right to be. But I couldn't risk showing any strange en…
while my husband was here monitoring me with an eagles' eye. So I th…
the flawless fake smile and played along with this unexpected mom…
"Let me go get rid of her, I'll be right back." I said
"Alright, I gotta go piss anyway."

…artificial smile turned into an enraged stillness once he closed the bathroom door l…
him. Ebony was laughing loudly at the T.V. when I walked back into t…
room. I picked up the remote and turned off the T.V., stopping her la…

"Trust me; I got a whole lot more than that." She said walking towards me with
her hand on her hip, the black woman's' stance again.
"What is that supposed to mean?" I asked
"Nothing, just know that you aint gotta worry about me no more."

bed her shoes and raced out of my house with her shoes and raced out of my hou
anger in each step.   I quickly ran after her and stopped her from getting

baby, I sorry. Its just that you can't be coming to my house unexpectedly and shi
my man was home, so how did you expect me to react?" I explaine

"Okay, I was fucked up for just showing up like that—but treating me the
way you did was uncalled for." She whined
"Goddammit Ebony!" I yelled "What the fuck do you want from me?"
"All I want, and have always ever wanted is you. I want you to be
mine and mine alone, I just want you."
"So what are you saying?"

She folded her arms and smacked her lips.
"It's either me, or Latrell."

aust have been sent down from the heavens for not taking all of these opportuniti
her in the mouth. But with all the sin that I was in I probably wouldn't even get a
past the pearly gates. I looked at her up and down then back to her blank
seriousness. I couldn't believe this shit was happening to me right now.
tried blinking my eyes a few times to see if I would wake up out of this dr
was slowly turning into my worst nightmare. I felt myself about to give i
threat, so I straightened my posture, and gave her the same seriousness
"Bye."
with my arms folded and anger trailing my footsteps as I walked back inside my h

Latrell

"I heard yelling, is everything cool?" I asked, out of curiosity.
"Everything's cool, she's just going through some things in her life right
now so I'm just tryna be a good friend."
She let out a huge sigh and looked at me apologetically
you wanna save what little time of our quality time night we have left?" she asked s

u know what baby, it's been a long day and I'm dog tired." I said, and it was the tr
e and ebony's fling I was left tired and empty. I no longer got the adrenaline that
received from my sin, my guilt weighed heavily on my soul. Only I coul
burden that I thought I was strong enough to carry. I took my wife's' hand
her to the bedroom slowly, my dick was sore and worn out so I couldn't w
more normal pace. I laid in my bed and contemplated on my next move
saving myself as well as my marriage. I didn't want to lose Darius' sexy a
wife's bomb ass pussy—this is beginning to get more complicated than I e

Alisha

uldn't sleep all night, tosses and turns made up for my lack of rest that night. I ev
tried to play with Latrells dick, hoping it would rise and give me somet
to make me go to sleep to, but the pillow Latrell had placed between
legs prevented me from even getting a passing glance. By the time my
closed my alarm clock was already hollering at me to wake me up.

got dressed, gave Latrell a kiss on the forehead and hit the road. I got to Starbuc
earlier that I usually did so the cheery woman with the big smile behi
the counter didn't have my order ready to go. When I first started drin
starbucks the woman behind the counter scared me, she smiled all the
and had a really high-pitched voice, even though my homegirls told me
Starbucks was the bomb, if I was going to start acting like the crazy la
behind the counter just from drinking the stuff then you could have

despite my fear, I envied her greatly. All of these years I've entangled myself in so
shit that made my toes curl, legs shake, and eyes roll to the back of r
head—but nothing that gave me a general happiness, a unique sunshi
a permanent joy. I got my order and walked towards the door.

"Thank you, have a nice day Alisha!" The cashier yelled
"Thank you, you too." I said, embarrassed
So ashamed of myself, I had been coming to this Starbucks for years, and I
hadn't even taken the time out to remember name.

"Oh I will." She responded
ed to my car and drove of to work, hoping that I would have a nice day for a cha

Latrell

I woke up about 10:30 that morning at the sound of my cell phone.
"Huh?" I said, answering my phone groggily.
'Whassup daddy?" Darius spoke
"Sleeping, whatchu want?"

I tried my hardest not to sound as irritated and tired as I felt, but the last
few days had been crazy and I had planned on spending my off day resting
in preparation for more of whatever my life had planned for me.

"How about I come over and wake you up?" He asked.

"You doin' a hell of a good job at that right now." I said with my eyes still shut.

"Since you already up then let me come through." He asked
"And do what?"
"I don't know, chill, talk, and watch T.V. it's up to you."

My eyes opened wide and my dick rose to attention, he hadn't said anything
sexual but my mind took the liberty to wander and get creative. I sat up
on my headboard and watched my dick as it stared back at me.

 about I kiss your neck, lick your nipples, and you suck my dick." I spoke with a

 at the knocking on my door and rushed to it, hearing my dick slap my stomach
I laughed and flipped my phone closed once I looked through the peephole. I o
 let Darius inside. He went straight to my bedroom and stripped down to his bo

"What gave you an idea like this?" He asked.

walked towards him and watched him tremble as I kissed his G-spot. He laid on
k as I slowly slid his boxer briefs off. I lifted his muscular legs and fingered him g
wing his moisture to make my fingers entrance more free. I licked my lips and qu

Alisha

I got to my desk to see another questioning crowd around my workspace; I let out
a fake cough to let my presence be known. I rolled my eyes as they scattered back
to their desks as if nothing was wrong. Four teddy bears and a bouquet of red roses
decorated my desk. I sat down with water-filled eyes and searched for the card.

'Because you deserve it...'

Everyday I fell in love with that man, and ever night I disgraced our title as
man and wife. Once again I couldn't resist the urge to call him.

It rang two times before it was answered.

"Hello?" A strange voice answered
"Who is this?" I asked, raising my voice slightly.

"You called here so tell me who you want to speak to?!?" he said

"Get Latrell on the phone now!" I demanded,

were watching me but my anger was high enough to ignore all of their judgments

"Oh, so you must be the wife. I've never got the chance to meet
you but I do have one thing to say to you."
"What the fuck are you talking about, and where the fuck is
my husband?" I said, interrupting his sentence.

"Aye bitch, calm down, he's in the shower. But before I hang this phone up in your
face please remember this—if I can't have him, then you won't either."

My heart crashed at the sound of the click.

up and saw my co-workers studying my emotionless and confused expressions as

my belongings, and walked to my car, imagining what more hell I've gotten mys

Latrell

I stared at Darius as he held the cordless phone in his hand and an accomplished
smirk on his face. I heard every word he said to my wife on the phone, and couldn
decipher what to do next. She was more than likely on her way to the hose now,
I was too mentally worn out to deal with the situation in it's' entirety.

I wrapped the towel tightly around my waist and walked towards him as
he walked backwards, eventually backing into the kitchen counter. He
dropped the phone and the battery slid under the refrigerator.

w could you?" I asked, forcing back tears at the thought of what I was at stake of

"I need you to love me." He said

"So this is how you do it?"
"It's not what it seems."
"Then what is it?"

"It's the perfect solution Latrell."
"Solution to what?"
"The solution to all of our problems."
There is only one real problem that I've had." I spoke while walking to my bedroo

"And what's that?" He said, following me

"Fucking with you."

d to my knees once he got the courage to push me. After regaining my balance, I
ght hook to remember. He rose to his feet, catching a left right combination as he
d dropped; my dick was swinging every which way as my fists connected to whate
Darius' body that I could reach. He rushed out of my home after knocking
down a few family pictures off my wall, and slammed the door shut.

tly heard the garage lift and Alisha's' car pull in. I looked down to see me still in

Alisha

dn't get out of my car right away; I sat there for a minute with my head on the ste
eel, contemplating my approach on this situation. I didn't feel as though it was w
it to make a scene so I decided to approach the situation calmly and smoothly.

"Who the fuck answered my phone!" I screamed at my husband,
fumbling attempting to cover his naked body.

"Baby –I."
"Don't baby me; I'm a grown ass woman!"
"I'm trying to explain--."
"Stop explaining and start answering!"

ked into his bloodshot eyes and balled my fists. I wasn't going to hit him, but I th
t it—thought about giving it to him one good time right in the mouth, hoping it
ge him to talk, to give me the answers to the many questions I had stored inside.
t to grab my purse from the floor that I dropped on the way in until my cell phon

Latrell

e looked at the phone as it lit up in our faces. I thought about bending down and
ing it up for her, but I was already in the dog house with my wife, didn't want to
g sent to the pound at this point. She picked up her stuff along with the flashing
ne and walked back to her car. A flashback of the text message she received a whi
ck from her mother tossed itself around in my head—but she was already gone an
out the door before I could form the words to the questions I wanted answered.

t out a deep sigh of relief and fell to the floor, realizing I was holding my breath th
e time my wife was here. I shut my eyes tightly to keep from shedding the tears t
esperately wanted to fall. This was no time to show any emotion about somethin
r really cared about until now. I got up and filled the rest of my day with screami
nching, and puking—trying my hardest to destroy my conscience, but no success.

Alisha

...d out of the garage and sped my way to the Neonopolis, I figured I would go catch
...omething to eat before I lost grip of my sanity all together. I parked in the car gara...
...re all windows were up. My eyes caught a glimpse of my purse leaning over the p...
...t to my surprise there were the mysterious silk underwear staring at me, somewhat
...e in the face. I giggled and tossed them in the backseat, not caring where they lan...

...wasn't on Latrell, didn't want to know what was going on and didn't care. I wasn't
...Ebony and whatever the fuck she was up to. I figured that I was wasting too much
...eople, at the moment Alisha was only worried about Alisha. I gathered my shit an...
...g towards the elevator with my fists balled and my compassion dissolved. I kept n...
..., looking straight ahead as I got there and pushed the button, so focused on my de...
...didn't realize my finger wasn't the only one on the button. I looked at the finger t...
...mine and followed it up to its' thick forearms and muscle-bound biceps, up to its
...o its' hypnotizing brown eyes. He was a gorgeous peanut-butter complected man.
...his twenties I would assume, but he carried himself so maturely, which perceived h...
...His eyelashes were long and lips were full, and his smile was perfect. I licked my...
...my finger back, thinking to myself that if angels existed, he definitely had to have...

...He said, snatching his finger back and placing it in his mouth. "You shocked me

..., I didn't mean to." I whispered, afraid that I possibly wasn't attractive enough fo...

"Don't trip—it ain't your fault, blame static electricity."

We giggled for a moment and stared at each other.

'DING'

...ened my mouth to say more but the arriving elevator stopped my attempt. I walk...

"What movie are you going to see?" He asked giving me no eye contact.

"This new movie called 'The Hills Have Eyes.' It's supposed to be
scary but I never believe what the previews say."

I took a deep breath and shifted my weight to my right side. He licked
his beautiful lips, making my pussy drip as he spoke.

at's cool, I'm gonna wait until I get up there and see what movies are playing first

evator stopped and I gave him a wave goodbye as I walked to the line to purchase
t pained me to give him such an early goodbye, to think that that could've been t
I would ever see such a beautiful example of a man. That is, until he followed me

Latrell

l I were supposed to be meeting at my house tonight but he wasn't answering his p
fter the 5th call and took a power nap. Once I got up I tried calling a few dozen m
But only got his voicemail…

Alisha

"Don't you think you might wanna answer your phone?" I
said, making my way to the concession stand.

ushed ignore on his cell phone and smiled, hypnotizing me for the nth time toni

"Not while I'm tryna spit game." He said, standing behind me in line.

never did tell me what movie you were going to see." I said, paying for my medi
rn and large coke. I struggled for a minute carrying my snacks, I knew I should I
n a small because the way Neonopolis makes them, a medium is damn near a lar

"I know." He said, moving forward to order himself something.

idn't wait for him, waiting for him would insinuate me wanting him to follow me
pite the fact that I wanted him to; I sure as hell wasn't going to let him know tha

nade my way to the dimly lit movie theatre and took my seat towards the back, a
other people. I never liked sitting next to other people in movie theatres, especia
lack people who have a habit of talking to the movie screen as if it will talk back.

there early enough to catch a few of the previews and get comfortable. My comf
vel dropped and entered into pleasure as he walked in. He had popcorn in one
nd, and in the other a large soda with his lips wrapped firmly around the straw.
ik down in my seat hoping he wouldn't spot me blushing. He looked around the
theatre before walking up the flight of steps to get to where I was sitting.

"Shit, he saw me…" I said to myself

I started getting back in my seat and looked at him.

"Nothing." I spoke "I thought you didn't know what movie you were going to see." I said, dusting the popcorn and God knows what else off of my pants.

"I didn't, but then I met a fine ass girl who talked me into one."

I smiled at his corky comment and nibbled on a piece of popcorn, watching the preview trailer of some new movie that was soon to be in theatres.

"Are you from here?" He asked, making my heart skip a beat.

"Yeah, born and raised. You?" I asked, still overwhelmed by how fine this man wa

"Naw, I'm originally from Mississippi, but I've been in Vegas since I was 18."

Damn,
Sexy and country, if there weren't any people in this theatre I would have fucked
him right there. But I was having fun getting to know him better.

"What school did you graduate from?" He asked.
"Cheyenne High School."

"What was your favorite subject?"
"Science…yours?"
"Math. Which science was your favorite? Earth Science? Biology? Physics?"

"Chemistry." I responded.

h you mean like the chemistry we have?" He said as I turned and connected eyes
the man who made me lose all knowledge of my husband in less than an hour.

ped my soda and sat up in my seat, showing off the sexy arch in my back and sm

"So what do you look for in a woman?" I asked.

in a deep breath inhaling his sweet smelling cologne, and placed my hand on his

"What's your name?" I asked
"Darius, but you can call me D."

"Okay, 'D'…well my name is Alisha and I'm about to keep it so real with you."

He smiled and raised his right eyebrow as I led him up to the very
back of the theatre, leaving our snacks behind.

We sat down and I lifted up both armrests and pressed my lips against his.

"I wanna fuck." I said, clutching his stiff dick.

At first I felt afraid to fuck this man in such a public place, but my chances
of ever meeting a man equal to his beauty was slim to none. So I took him
while I had him within my grasp—and his dick in my mouth.

lutched his balls and deep-throated his dick, listening to him and the seats squeal
as he squirmed. I couldn't believe what I was doing and felt my guilt creeping
p behind me, but my sense of reality, and the angel on my shoulder was ignored
once again as he laid me down, worshipping my breasts with his tongue.

uilty, I couldn't take it anymore and tried to get up and end it while I had the cha
ny panties were off before the 'please silence your cell phones' sign was on the scre

ased his dick inside and stroked me as if we were the only two people in the theat
e sucked on my neck as I bit my lower lip—to keep from screaming his name…

Latrell

I paced my room in anger and confusion. I called Darius at
least fifty times and had yet to receive one back.

wanted to talk about the fight we had, and couldn't leave things the way they were

wife hadn't been back home since she left in a rage earlier, my mind began to wan

I sat on my living room floor and drowned myself in my thoughts
of where my wife and my lover could possibly be….

Alisha

Faster and faster he stroked, knocking down any remaining walls my pussy had.

…g stroked and nibbled my neck as my come started to flow out of me like a mens… … Fast then slow, grinding then coming, in and put, I rode, he came, he ate, I suck…

…Over and over again I disgraced my husband with every nut I busted, and had the … …ve to wonder why my life was what it was. For a moment my guilt began to reve… itself and that annoying angel on my shoulder would try and intervene.

…rs fell from my eyes out of disgust. This nigga could lay some serious pipe but all …creams and subtle moans were meant for Latrell. I pushed his upper body from m… …tried to sit up, but he held my wrists and continued to grind. He kissed me hard… …d I pushed him up again, this time making him fall back two seats away from me…

I searched for my clothes and got dress as quietly as I could without disturbing those who were actually watching the movie.

…quinted and guided my hands across the floor making sure I didn't leave anything …ehind. My hands touched something cold and I picked it up to see what it was…

…It was his cell phone; it must have dropped out when I pushed him off of me.

…he battery was slightly out of place so I popped it back in and handed it to him.

"Here's your phone." I said,

…hing him get himself dressed, I could tell by the look on his face hoe bad he wan… …uss me out, but he obviously also didn't want to interrupt any of the other viewe…

et me speak. I balled my fists and eased out of the theatre without Darius knowing

As my husbands cell phone number flashed before my eyes....

Latrell

hrew my cell on the passenger seat of my car as I sped my way down the street. M
100th call gave me an unsteady feeling in the pit of my stomach, letting me know
that whatever was about to happen wasn't going to be anything positive.

'st stop was her job, thinking maybe she stayed at work longer or had some extra f
do. But her desk was empty and nothing was there except a bouquet of black rose

ced to her desk and covered my nose as the strong smell of spray paint filled the o
The paint dripped from the flowers and onto the card attached to the stems, it rea

'Because you deserve it...'

card in my back pocket and raced back to my car, my next stop was to Darius' ho

Alisha

was home when I got there so I took the liberty of searching my home from top t[o]

[...]d over dressers, and knocked down lamps in search of the answers I so desperately [...] I fell on the living room floor out of exhaustion from my rampage. I breathed heavily and stared at the phone I stole from Darius.

I figured since I couldn't find any evidence within my own home, then maybe at least I could get some closure from my own husband.

Latrell

m got tired from knocking on Darius' door. I banged and kicked, ignoring the cu
₁ the other tenants in the complex. I got back into my car and caught my breath.
₋mped to the sound of my cell phone and saw a text message from Darius, it read:

> *'We need to talk, meet me at your house…'*

I threw the phone back on the passenger side and made my
way home to make myself presentable for him.

The tears kept flowing when I pressed send.

I wasn't sure if he would come but I was at the point where I would even kill
for the explanation I knew in my heart I deserved. I picked myself up and
sat quietly on the sofa, waiting for my husband to get home…

Latrell

I got out the car and walked towards my front door....

Alisha

I closed my eyes as his footsteps clicked and clacked in my ears…

Latrell

I unlocked the door....

the doorknob turned and watched my husband gasp with stains of tears covering

"Baby, I---."

"Who is he?" I asked, testing to see how far he would allow his lies to stretch.

"Who is who?" he started "Why is the house all fucked up? Did we get robbed or something?" he interrogated.

"Who…is he!" I asked once more, clutching the edge of the sofa.

"I don't know what you are talking about." He said folding his arms.

ok out Darius' cell phone and scrolled down into his contacts menu and pressed '

id the phone to his feet and watched him jump as his cell phone rang in his pock

Latrell

"Fuck." I thought to myself as my long kept secret literally rang in my face.

re what to do or how to go about doing it, but I did know that being in my wife's
lping the situation along at all. She had fire in her eyes and paint in her heart, fo
I could honestly say that I was intimidated by my wife. Which was why I tried to

I swung open the door and ran outside…

Alisha

My guts nearly dropped out of my stomach when I saw Darius' rugged, sweaty an
gloomy frame at the front door with a gun pointed at my husband's head.

nce beautiful man that I had just fucked, looked as if he had vacationed in hell an

iought you loved me." Darius said trembling with the gun still facing Latrells' fore

everything for you and still chose that bitch over me." He said, this time pointing
I watched Latrell as his hands were raised in surrender and I could feel my blood
or a split second I didn't care if Darius pulled the trigger or not, either way hell wo
over my life. I was hurting, and he needed to feel it too. I had to make sure he fe

IH SHIT!" Latrell yelled once I ripped his eyebrow piercing from his face, watchi
e blood stained the carpet below, thus marking my inbred anger and disgust for h

"Bitch!" Darius yelled as he slapped me across the living room with the gun.

I landed on a piece of broken lamp and screamed out in agony. I slowly rose
to my feet and pulled the lamp fragment out of my right thigh.

"Quit it D." Ebony said walking in the front door, also with a gun in her hand.

"That bitch is mine…"

Latrell

grabbed a cut up t-shirt from off the floor and held it to my face to soak up some
the blood. Reality hadn't fully set in on me and the pain I was feeling was beyon
ense. I watched in shocked as my wife trembled at the gun aimed at her skull. Fo
oment, I felt that if Ebony had pulled the trigger then the pain I had already caus
her would die along with her. But I was the one who was in the wrong, not her.

I deserved death…being cold-hearted towards her was uncalled for.

haven't you called me Alisha?" Ebony started "Too busy with your bitch ass husba

She said staring at me with the same tear-filled eyes as the time I
fucked her senseless right where she was standing.

I couldn't believe what I was seeing, wouldn't believe what I was hearing, I
didn't want to believe any of this, but I knew I had no choice…

Alisha

"Shit."
I thought to myself.

enraged by discovering my husbands' infidelities that I almost forgot about my ov

"You think you can play games with people emotions like this?" She said
Trembling and sweating just as hard as Darius was.

Ebony what the fuck is going on?" I said, shaking from the increasing pain in my

fuck up! One day you love me and the next day you kickin' me out of your crib, bi

tuned her out and looked at Latrell who was more focused on tending to his wou
than listen to Ebony vent and run her mouth about our secretive relationship.

now what was about to go down, but I did know that I wasn't going to be made i

ped over to Ebony as fast as I could and knocked the pistol from her hand. She g
y hair and kneed me in my groin. As I knelt on the floor in pain I came back wit
p object from the floor right into her foot. I rose back up and stuck her in the m
rrupting her screams with my diamond wedding ring to her jaw, the ring I barely

trell took the blood soaked t-shirt and wrapped it around Darius' neck, swinging
m left to right. I held Ebony down on the floor and began rubbing her face deep
ie carpet. She managed to push me off of her and get up to wipe some of the brol
glass off of her skin. Me and Ebony locked eyes as my husband and Darius wrestl
on the side of us, knocking down every piece of African art in our living room.

at me with full force and socked me in the chest; I stumbled back and caught my
It was really time to get in this bitch's ass…

Latrell

"Damn."

hought to myself when I saw Alisha give Ebony a clean two-hit combo to the face

Darius reached up and poked me in the eye, giving him the chance to wiggle
out of my grip, I stumbled backwards into the wall and broke the painting of
an African man and woman hugging in an almost skin tight embrace.

eye and once my vision returned I was once again staring at the tip of a heavily l
own at the broken painting as it laid there lifeless, almost as if it was telling me so

Letting me know what the consequences were because of my selfish and sinful
desires. The broken painting represented me and my wife's future.
Broken, and split down the middle.

skin tight embrace now ripped apart, loose and fragmented. I was going to lose
onight and I wasn't ready to deal with that large reality, there was nothing I coul
e to make everything better, what was done was done, and couldn't be taken bac
But I could still show her, let her know that my love for her was never artificial.

So I raised my head and stared back at the gun pointed in between my eyes,
The gun which now represented my destiny…

Everything in our living room felt like it was frozen in time,

Ebony and I panted and gasped as we stared at the men.

Latrell, now standing firm and confident, Darius…still nervous,
and yet bold enough to keep his finger on the trigger.

"Why?" Darius asked, crying streams of tears.

"Why what/" Latrell asked, showing no sign of emotion or remorse on his face.
"Why would you treat me like somebody's play toy huh?"
"Darius, I didn't---."
ıt the fuck up! I'm talkin' now!" he yelled, this time placing the gun on Latrells' te

"You've been talkin' for too long now, it's my turn. Everything was always about
you and life, but you didn't give two shits about me did you? Did you?"
"Darius, I did care about you, but I never loved you."
"Why?" he asked, pouting

"I'm married to the one person I love." I responded

t sure didn't mean too much when you was sucking' my dick and eating' my ass d

I couldn't believe what I was hearing, I ran to the kitchen sink and vomited
at the thought of my husband giving head to some dude, and then kissing
me, leaving who knows what kind of fluids on my taste-buds.

I fell to my knees and wept, realizing that I was guilty of the same crime towards
my husband-- leaving who knows what kind of fluids on his taste-buds—and also
sleeping with the man who now caused me so much disgust at the moment.

Darius speak of a 'Cumming party' they once had in the sink I just threw up in.

I listened, learned, and vomited some more, out of disgust
towards my husband, as well as towards myself…

Latrell

"And then that time you ate me out the night before your wedding, and then--."

been going on and on and on about us for the last thirty minutes, not once did I
n, I could only sit there and relive the truth to my lies—but a man can only take s

"Darius shut the hell up! What the fuck are you doing this shit
for huh? What is all this shit really about?"

wered his gun down and walked towards Ebony to help her up, I walked over to
l tried to do the same but she yanked her arm away from me and got up on her ov

Alisha

"Don't touch me nigga." I said

rell wasn't on my good list at the moment, but we did agree on one thing. We bo
perately wanted to know their motives behind doing some off the wall shit like th

I folded my arms and faced them both.

"For real though, what the fuck is all this shit about?"

Latrell

"You have what I've always wanted Latrell." Darius said.

"And what's that?" I asked

"Love…"

He shifted the gun to his right hand and walked towards me.

…ad love and I wanted the same for us, but unfortunately you had more love for y…
…r you lover, I'm fed up Latrell, I want you for me, not me and some bitch of a wo…
…n't know affection if it bit her in the ass, I love you Latrell, I want to be your ever…

"My wife is my everything!" I screamed
"No she's not! I AM!! ME! ME! ME! ME! ME! ME!"

"Darius stop!" I shouted trying to calm his tantrum.

"Fuck you Latrell, you are my man, not hers, so who the fuck is it going to
be huh? Me? Or her? And you don't have too long to answer me."

I looked at my wife and then looked at my lover, then looked at my lover
some more, then focused my attention back on my wife.

"Damn."
I thought to myself…

Alisha

"You're fucking kidding me."

I thought to myself as I saw my husband shift his attention from me to that faggot. This motha-fucka actually had to *think* about who he was going to choose. You would think that the so-called love your life would be the obvious choice.

"You've got to be fucking kidding me." I thought to myself again.

I'm the one who loves him…

Latrell

He's the one who holds me...

Alisha

I'm the one who feeds him…

Latrell

She's the one who understands me…

Alisha

I'm the one who comforts him…

Latrell

And he's the one who fills that void, the one to be there for me when she's not....

Alisha

I'm the one who needs him in my life…

Latrell

But she's the one who I gave the ring to.

I thought this would be such an obvious choice.
"Oh Shit." I thought to myself

ow could my pleasure override my love? How could I let sinful desires take contro
my reality, and in return destroy a marriage and a home in less than three hours?

"Time's up." He said,
Raising the gun once again to my forehead. "Who is it going to be?"

I looked at my wife who was staring at the floor, than back to my pissed off
lover. I myself surrendered to my emotions and the tears began to flow.

you from the jump that I would never leave my wife for you, and I still stick to n

"Oh you mean like the vow to stay faithful?" He asked.
"Shit." I thought.

ght, but my goal was to have my slate wiped clean once the night was over, throw
ness of my past, but it didn't help my situation when the subject continues to be

lly are a fucked up person for this baby." He said, now crying ten times harder th

it it's cool, if I can't have you, there's no point for me here, I guess I should leave

He turned his head toward the weeping Ebony and smiled.

"Tell momma that I love her, and I'm sorry."

I raised my eyebrow in confusion.

Alisha

"You have got to be fucking kidding me."

I repeated to myself in my head.

dn't surprise me though, hoe ass bitch wanted my man from the first time she saw
It didn't surprise me in the least, but it did disgust me, I vomited
a little bit more, this time inside of my mouth.

Once again, for me and my husband…

Latrell

"Oh Shit."

I thought again.

ed his head back towards me and raised the gun to my head. I balled my fist and
tightly, ready to prove that my love for Alisha was alive, even if I had to die to pr

"Do you love me?" Darius asked
"No." I said with my eyes tightly shut.
"Did you care for me?"
"Yes."
"Can you leave her for me?"
"No."
"Please?"
"No."
s there anything…anything I can do to have you for myself, and leave her alone?"
"No, absolutely not."
"Will you miss me?" he said…

"What?"

'POW!'

said out loud, as I watched Darius' blood shoot in my face, and his body fall to t

"Oh Shit."

Alisha

"You've got to be fucking kidding me."

I thought as I wiped off some remains of what I assumed to be Darius' brain off of my arm. Ebony ran out of the door in tears, she just watched her brother blow his brains out; no one could stand to stomach something like that.

Half of me was remorseful and the other half was relieved. I was afraid at first, scared that she was going to run her mouth and spill the beans on our affair, but now with her gone my secret can last another day.

"You're fucking kidding me."

I continued to think to myself as I kneeled next to his now lifeless body, realizing that nothing about this was a joke…

Latrell

I kneeled beside my wife and wept with my mouth wide open in shock.

blood, along with my own, covered my face, hands and floor. Alisha showed no e
face, not because she didn't care, but probably hadn't let the situation sink in just

y hands upon his chest, hoping to find some sort of hope of him being alive, but

Just a poor, cold, heartbroken, love-seeking man, all of which he
was willing to give his life for in order to receive.

All of this, all of this turmoil caused by my dick and my ego. Never wanting to
answer to the truth and yet defending every lie. Never wanting to have dinner
with my wife, but I couldn't wait to eat Darius out all night long.

xtremely fucked up how a few measly moments of sin and satisfaction can destro
ns' mental state of mind, allowing chaos to roam free. But it's even more outstanc
believe that a persons' mind could be altered, even controlled to a certain degree.
hated what I did to my wife and would take it back if at all virtually possible.

ze that while my moments of constant dick sucking, and ass fucking, I was hurtir
ss. For much longer than a moment, I prolonged her suffering for far more than :
I got greedy with the pleasures of this world.

And that I believe---was my greatest sin…

Alisha

:ed up as I saw Latrell take the gun from Darius' limp hand and walked to the bac
; his feet as he swayed. I rose up and walked to the bathroom, tended to my woun
r, re-doing any individuals in my hair that were messed up during me and Ebony's

I splashed some cold water on my face to remove any dried
blood, and then stared at myself in the mirror.

"Damn I'm fine."

I said, caressing my curves, and worshipping my body.
I stripped, got in the shower and got dressed. I met Latrell on
the patio to get a last look at him before I left.

as lying back on the patios' swing, rocking back and forth, staring at the stars as h
I shook my head and let out a sigh of pity for my husband, then walked
to my car which was thoroughly keyed and scratched.

I shook my head again and got inside.

anted to avoid thinking about everything that had just taken place in my home, i
of vomiting again. But instead I laughed about how dreadfully unexpected it wa

n wondered how long my game would have lasted had I continued my fling with
I she kept her emotions aside, but I eventually lost all thought of Ebony and the r
cked, who was now a dead man on my living room floor, drowning in his own bl
he car and made my way to 'Hamburger Hut' to grab something to eat. I took n
and tucked it in my bra, making a mental note to go to the pawn shop later on t

l have made everything a lot better if Latrell would have told me what he was doi
ving to find out that way, I would have respected him more. It also would have b
: to tell him what I was up to as well I guess, but what he didn't know wouldn't h

…ot enough pages in the world to express my thanks to the many people who have
…n for my success. Just because your name isn't present…doesn't mean you didn't pl…

All I can say is…FINALLY!!! Lol

…e class of 2008 of Canyon Springs should know how long I have wanted to becom…
a writer, and by holding this book in your hands my dream is now a reality.

The creation of this story was pure imagination…no truth to
it unless you create a truth of your own…lol

…s story when I was 15 years old, and now four years later it finally has come into fi…
…question is why now? The simplest answer to that question without making you
…r is to say that the characters just weren't ready, in the beginning my imagination l…
…oung lady named Tanya, after speaking with her about the character I wanted her
…ped me in the face--- appalled that I asked how comfortable she felt about eating
After readjusting my jaw, my imagination gave me the great
pleasure of coming across a striking woman, Alisha.

Her body was out of this world and her eyes had no ounce of fear in them. I
knew then that she would be the one…we talked for months discussing
what kind of man she liked…and what she expected from him.
…atrell was the needle in the haystack of many men that Alisha liked, the girl was a
…ynpho…but that's neither here nor there. It wasn't the sexual side I was looking
for in the characters…I craved for the intent and true color of their soul…

…ad no doubt in my mind that with Alisha's ego, and Latrell's humble indecisivenes…
would be the perfect ingredients needed to make this story one to remember.

Quick Thank You's:

Thanks to my mother, for giving birth, creating a creator of creativities…lol
…on Springs High School class of 2008! I remember passing out pages of stuff I wo…
…e down and let yall' read, it was all of your feedback that helped me perfect my cra…
…nd also to the teachers who saw me not paying attention in class because I was too…
…y writing…if it wasn't for yall I wouldn't have found the time! My grandma, (who…
…will never read this story…or any of the next ones) I promise your grandson is n…
…a freak…(wink)…I'm just a true spokesperson for one's imagination. Love you!
Auntie Valerie! Love youuuuuuu
Uncle Flap, stay out of trouble…love you
Uncle David, Danny Paul, TT Tammy, Janika, Brandon, Vondre'

My brothers and sisters, Vanessa, Chanelle, Lester Jr., Dominique, Sharnelle, Chri
Darius (NO RELATION TO THE STORY…SIMPLY COINCIDENCE..=^)
), Marcus, AJ, Maurice, I told you your lil' bro was gonna do it!!!

By: LeMario 'ZOKO' Allen

"Daddy wanna hear you scream." Romeo said while forcefully licking my pussy.

looked up and smiled as my facial expression gave away my feelings of enjoyment.
in and kissed his full lips that were glistening from getting a mouthful of my juic
ked my lips after our kiss, dwelling upon the taste of myself—damn I tasted good

"I'm ready for that dick daddy." I responded, looking deep into his hazel eyes.

d some crazy dominant fantasies and always demanded control in the bedroom. I
o refer to him as 'Daddy' or 'Papi' during intercourse. I suppose it made him feel
e—nonetheless, I say whatever, I get my nut either way, so if calling him a couple
his name made him feel good, the least I could for Romeo was be his submissive

He picked me up from the bed by my ass cheeks and held me close to
his chest, aggressively sucking on my breasts and neck.

"Damn Romeo, that's my spot!" I moaned.

d his head and raised an eyebrow, looking at me as if I just took a shit on his face
loosened and I dropped to the floor landing flat on my ass. I looked up and analy
gorgeous muscular frame and oozed wetness as I stared at the veins in his forearm

"What did you call me?" He asked raising up one side of his top lip.
"Romeo." I said, realizing that in the heat of passion I identified him
incorrextly, breaking one of his most important rules.

at are you supposed to be calling me?" He said, kneeling down holding his erect
ng me no eye contact whatsoever. I played along and taunted him with my own

"Ummm…" I said, pretending to catch a slight case of amnesia.

He caught me off guard and grabbed my neck, pinning me to the floor.
"Wrong answer bitch!" He screamed while thrusting his ten inch rod deep
inside me making me wish that 'daddy' was my first response.

deeper his dick lunged inside me—making my pussy squirt after each pump. Ne
d a dick tear my insides up as forcefully as Romeo did. If this were modern day
uld have had to say fuck the Capulets and the Montagues—romeo got some seric

ipped his silky hair and arched my back, grinding him as he drilled. Nothing bu

"Oh you tryna make me nut hoe?" He asked, breathing heavily.

"Fuck you bitch, I ain't nuttin' for you!"
"What?" I said with passion in my eyes.

He punched the floor again, this time pulling up some pieces of my
newly installed carpet and throwing it across the room.

"Fuck you bitch, I ain't nuttin' for you!" He said

I felt his knees begin to buckle.

'What?" I said, continually taunting him.

"I ain't…" He said
"What?"
"Fuck…you."
"I can't hear you daddy!"
"I…fuck…you…ain't."

He rose quickly to his feet and hovered over me with his dick in hand.

inna fuckin' nut!" He screamed as a hot sticky fluid shot into my hair, nose, eyes,
various other areas. I watched as he continued to jack off his dick as he stood ove

"Fuck you bitch!" He said, emptying another load of himself on me.

out another fifteen minutes the cycle repeated, he would stroke himself and decor
vith the results from his stroke. I would try to get up but the slight kick to my ril
give me gave me second thoughts. So I just lay there, watching him, enduring my

self is a crazy thing, but it made me feel good to give it—as well as receive. Rom
ttle unnaturally dominant in the bedroom but all I knew was…he liked it, and I